JIMMY ZANGWOW'S

OUT-OF-THIS-WORLD

Moon·Pie

ADVENTURE

JIMMY ZANGWOW'S
OUT-OF-THIS-WORLD
Moon · Pie
ADVENTURE

My Spaceship

steer...

Nobble

drawn by
Jimmy Zangwow

STORY AND PICTURES BY
TONY DiTERLIZZI

Simon & Schuster Books for Young Readers

this book, cover to cover, is for Angela — t.d.

ACKNOWLEDGMENTS: Chattanooga Bakery, Inc., was founded in the early 1900s, and within a decade the Tennessee company was offering more than two hundred different baked items. In 1917, the bakery developed a new treat called the MOONPIE®. Popular response was so enormous that by the late 1950s, the bakery was producing nothing but the chocolate marshmallow double-decker sandwich. During the early 1970s, an impressionable young artist named Tony DiTerlizzi had his first taste of the treat. The rest—as they say—is history.

Special thanks to Chattanooga Bakery, Inc., for the use of the MOONPIE® name. MOONPIE® is a registered trademark of Chattanooga Bakery, Inc., and is used here with permission. For more information visit www.moonpie.com on the World Wide Web.

Special jumping june bug thanks to Rebecca Gomez, Cindi, and Mommy "Dearest" DeFrancis. And a huge Grimble Grinder hug to Kevin for helping me make my dream come true.

SIMON & SCHUSTER BOOKS FOR YOUNG READERS. An imprint of Simon & Schuster Children's Publishing Division, 1230 Avenue of the Americas, New York, New York 10020. Copyright © 2000 by Tony DiTerlizzi. All rights reserved including the right of reproduction in whole or in part in any form. SIMON & SCHUSTER BOOKS FOR YOUNG READERS is a trademark of Simon & Schuster. Book design by Anahid Hamparian. The text for this book is set in 17-point Venetian. The illustrations are rendered in watercolor, gouache, and colored pencil. Printed in Hong Kong 10 9 8 7 6 5 4 3 2 1   Library of Congress Cataloging-in-Publication Data   DiTerlizzi, Tony.   Jimmy Zangwow's out-of-this-world, Moon Pie adventure / by Tony DiTerlizzi. — 1st ed.   p.   cm.   Summary: When Jimmy's mother won't let him have any Moon Pies for a snack, he takes a trip to the moon to get some.   ISBN 0-689-82215-4   [1. Space flight to the moon—Fiction. 2. Moon Pies—Fiction. 3. Science fiction.]   I. Title.   PZ7.D629Ji 2000   [Fic]— dc21   98-16602   CIP   AC

first edition

One Tuesday afternoon Jimmy Zangwow asked his mom, "Can I *pleeaase* have some milk and a Moon Pie?"

"Of course not," his mom replied. "You'll ruin dinner. Now run outside and play."

"Aww, nuts!" Jimmy muttered as he stomped out his back door and climbed aboard his secret project.

"I wish I could go to the moon and get my own Moon Pies, but this junk jumbilee jalopy will never fly. . . ."

With that, the jalopy shook.

It rattled.

It battled to get off the ground.

"Holy macaroni!" Jimmy cried. He shut his eyes tight, and the jalopy rocketed up, up . . .

. . . and out of this world!

When Jimmy opened his eyes, he was high above the earth.

"Wow—I've never been this far from home." And he wondered if he could find his way back in time for dinner.

His stomach rumbled. Up ahead loomed the slumbering moon.

"Mmm! Moon Pies."

When Jimmy was close enough to the great Moon Pie maker in the sky, he roped him and climbed out of his jalopy. "Mr. Moon, can I please have some Moon Pies?"

Opening one eye, the old moon spoke, "What? You want french fries? Don't have any."

"Moon Pies!" shouted Jimmy.

"Fruit flies? Never seen one. . . ."

"No, Mr. Moon! I would like some MOON PIES!"

"Well, you don't have to yell," said the moon. "I'm not hard of hearing, y'know. Just a bit of cheese in my ears."

Jimmy took a deep breath and started again. "Mr. Moon, can I *pleeaase* have some Moon Pies?"

The moon gave Jimmy a long, thoughtful look.

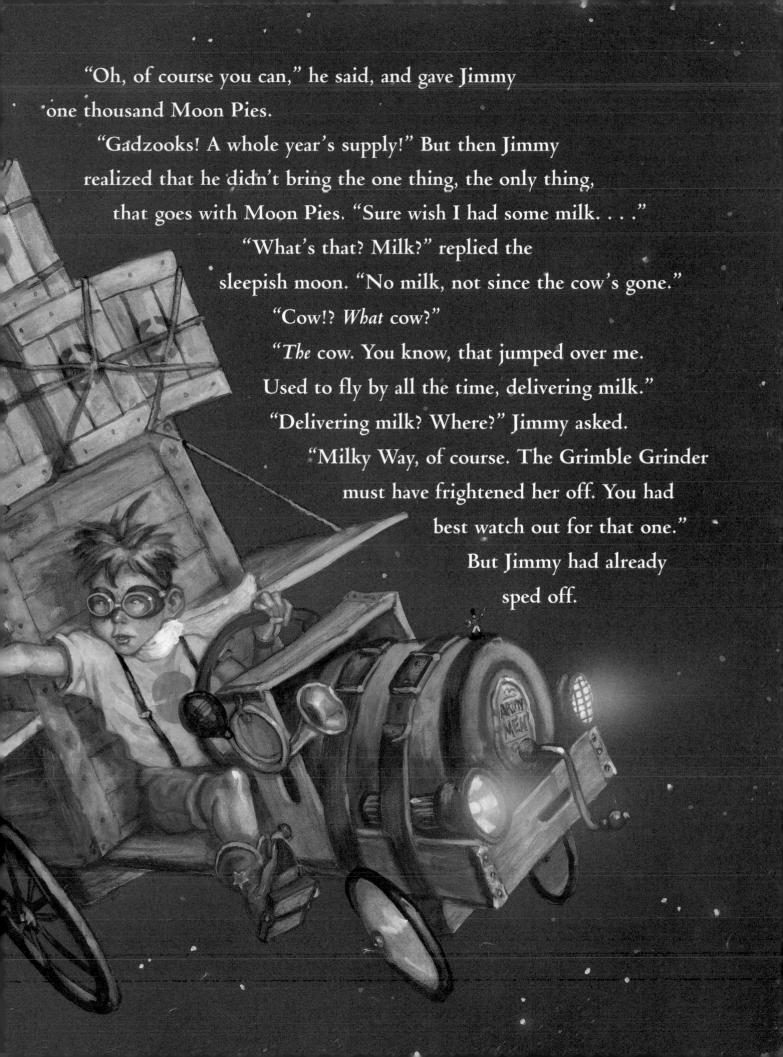

"Oh, of course you can," he said, and gave Jimmy
one thousand Moon Pies.

"Gadzooks! A whole year's supply!" But then Jimmy
realized that he didn't bring the one thing, the only thing,
that goes with Moon Pies. "Sure wish I had some milk. . . ."

"What's that? Milk?" replied the
sleepish moon. "No milk, not since the cow's gone."

"Cow!? *What* cow?"

"*The* cow. You know, that jumped over me.
Used to fly by all the time, delivering milk."

"Delivering milk? Where?" Jimmy asked.

"Milky Way, of course. The Grimble Grinder
must have frightened her off. You had
best watch out for that one."

But Jimmy had already
sped off.

In the Milky Way, Jimmy found gallons and quarts and pints of milk. He pulled out his net and was scooping up as much frosty, frothy stuff as he could when he heard the grumble.

RUMBLE-GRUMBLE!

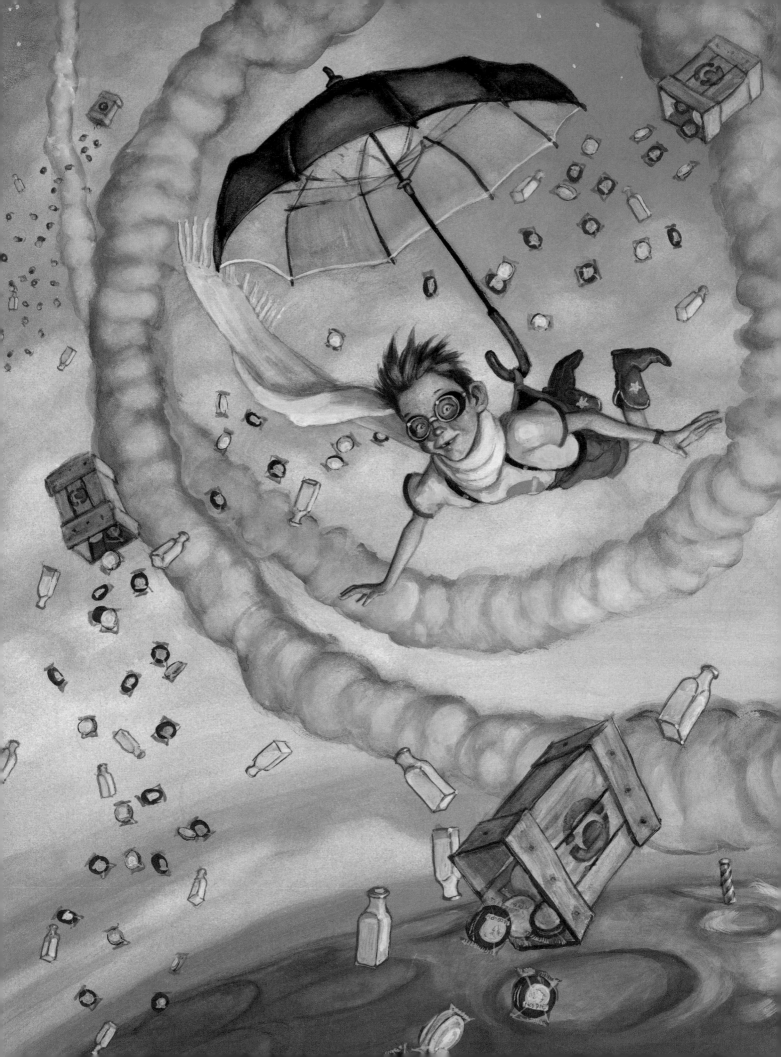

GRUMBLE-RUMBLE!

The grumble was *so loud* that it flipped the jalopy and sent Jimmy, his milk, and all one thousand Moon Pies tumbling straight down . . .

. . . to Mars where Jimmy landed in a crowd of Mars Men.

"It is raining milk!" they called out together. "It is snowing Moon Pies. WE WANT MOON PIES!"

"Oh no." Jimmy sighed. "How many of you are there?"

"Nine hundred ninety-nine."

"Nine hundred ninety-nine! That only leaves one for me!"

But then he saw all those hungry, little Mars-Men eyes and knew.

There wasn't any other way.

"All right, I'll share."

And the Martian milk-and-Moon-Pie feast began!

But before anyone could even take a bite, they heard:

RUMBLE-GRUMBLE,
GRUMBLE-RUMBLE.

All nine hundred ninety-nine Mars Men froze, and the ground
shook as the sound bounded forward.

RUMBLE-GRUMBLE,
GRUMBLE-RUMBLE.

"Jumping june bugs! What in the world is that?" Jimmy asked.

"It's the great Grimble Grinder!" the Mars Men exclaimed.

The big-bellied beastie groared and rowled.

RUMBLE-GRUMBLE, GRUMBLE-RUMBLE.

"He will eat us!" cried Mars Man Three-Sixty-Five. "We're tasty little nuggets in his gigantic eyes!"

"Eat us!" Jimmy said. "He can't do that! I'll miss my supper!"

He had to do something.

But what?

RUMBLE-GRUMBLE, GRUMBLE-RUMBLE.

Jimmy looked down at his hands.

"If you gotta eat something," he said, "eat this." And he held out a bottle of milk and his very last Moon Pie.

Grabbing the milk and Moon Pie, the Grimble Grinder gobbled up both and belched out loud.

"BUURRRRUPPP!"

Then that giant monster smiled—and spoke. "Thank you! Thank you! That was just what I needed. I was *sooo* hungry for *sooo* long that my belly rumbled and grumbled and growled. When I tried to ask for food, it spoke louder than I did. It frightened everyone away."

"You mean you don't want to eat us?" asked Jimmy.

"Oh goodness gracious, no! I just wanted a Moon Pie!"

Hearing this, the Mars Men cheered!

"Zip Pip Kaboodle! Zip Pip Kaboodle! Jimmy Zangwow has saved the day! Zip Pip Kaboodle!"

But now, *Jimmy's* stomach rumbled. He was starving! He looked at his watch.

"Six past! I'm gonna be late for dinner!"

And the jalopy was all crashed up and smashed!

"I'll never get home in time now!" groaned Jimmy.

"Yes, you will. We will help you," said Mars Man Three-Sixty-Five.

And, just like that, the Mars Men gathered up all of the Moon Pie wrappers and stitched them together to make a GIANT MOON-PIE-WRAPPER BALLOON!

"Now what?" Jimmy asked. "To make it work we need hot air!"

His watch read a quarter past.

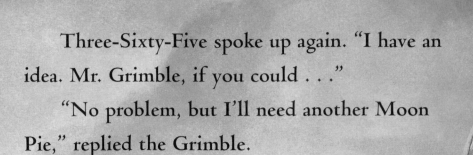

Three-Sixty-Five spoke up again. "I have an idea. Mr. Grimble, if you could . . ."

"No problem, but I'll need another Moon Pie," replied the Grimble.

All nine hundred ninety-nine Mars Men shouted, "Take mine!"

The Grimble Grinder gobbled up every single Moon Pie. Then, he seized the balloon, opened his mouth wide, and . . .

"BRAAARRRUUUPPP!!!!"

(He burped so hard that Moon Pies blew out of his ears and landed miles away!)

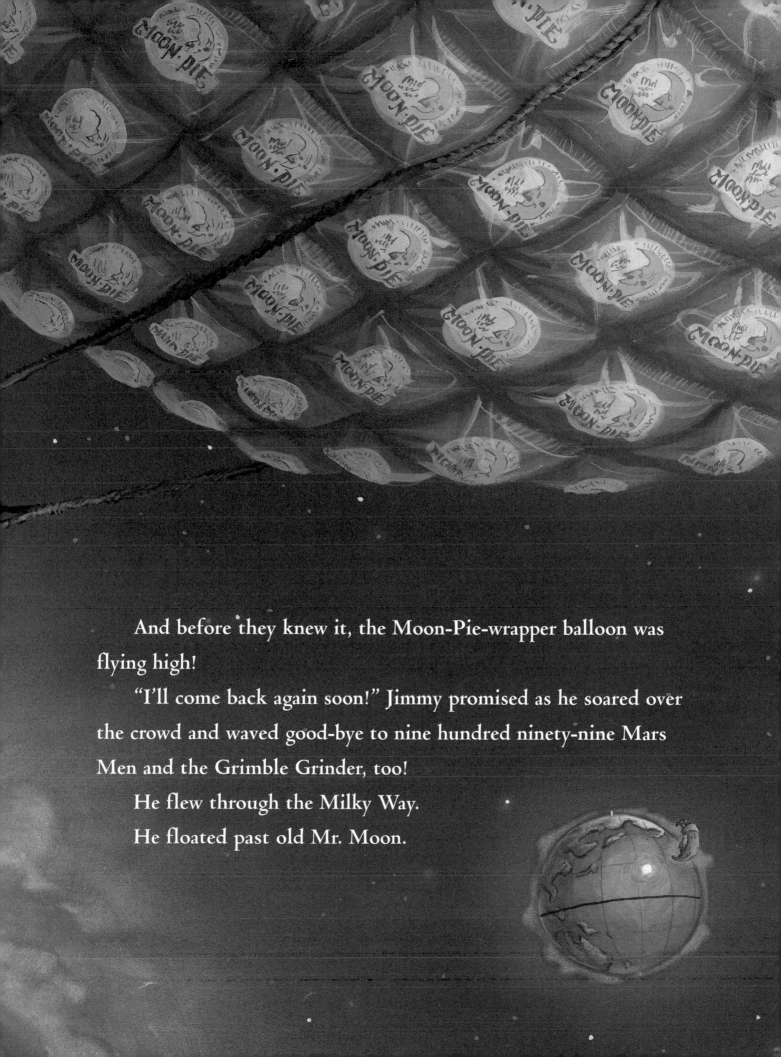

And before they knew it, the Moon-Pie-wrapper balloon was flying high!

"I'll come back again soon!" Jimmy promised as he soared over the crowd and waved good-bye to nine hundred ninety-nine Mars Men and the Grimble Grinder, too!

He flew through the Milky Way.

He floated past old Mr. Moon.

And he landed in his backyard just in time to hear his mom call, "Jimmy! Dinner!"

Jimmy was so hungry that he ate up every last bit, even though it was brussels-sprout-noodle-bean casserole . . .

. . . and when he was done, he got a Moon Pie for dessert.